THE GUARDIANS

TOOTHIANA
—— part three ——

Panic Sets In

WILLIAM JOYCE

Atheneum Books for Young Readers
NEW YORK • LONDON • TORONTO • SYDNEY • NEW DELHI

Atheneum Books for Young Readers • An imprint of Simon & Schuster Children's Publishing Division • 1230 Avenue of the Americas,
New York, New York 10020 • This book is a work of fiction. Any references to historical events, real people, or real places are used
fictitiously. Other names, characters, places, and events are products of the author's imagination, and any resemblance to actual events
or places or persons, living or dead, is entirely coincidental. • Copyright © 2012 by William Joyce • Rise of the Guardians TM & ©
2012 DreamWorks Animation, LLC. "Pitch" character design and related elements used with permission. All rights reserved. • All rights
reserved, including the right of reproduction in whole or in part in any form. • ATHENEUM BOOKS FOR YOUNG READERS
is a registered trademark of Simon & Schuster, Inc. • Atheneum logo is a trademark of Simon & Schuster, Inc. • For information about
special discounts for bulk purchases, please contact Simon & Schuster Special Sales at 1-866-506-1949 or business@simonandschuster.
com. • The Simon & Schuster Speakers Bureau can bring authors to your live event. For more information or to book an event, contact the
Simon & Schuster Speakers Bureau at 1-866-248-3049 or visit our website at www.simonspeakers.com • Book design by Lauren Rille •
The text for this book is set in Adobe Jenson Pro. • The illustrations for this book are rendered in a combination of charcoal, graphite, and
digital media. • Manufactured in the United States of America 1012 OFF • 10 9 8 7 6 5 4 3 2 1 • CIP data for this book is available
from the Library of Congress. • ISBN 978-1-4424-7455-0

PREVIOUSLY, IN
TOOTHIANA,
A Queen Takes Flight,

KATHERINE'S WORRYING ABOUT HER friend Nightlight led to her taking a terrifying fall. It was only Nightlight's otherworldly flying speed that prevented utter disaster. He'd been able to catch her before she was badly hurt, but not before she knocked out her last baby tooth. This small loss, however, might just turn out to be a tremendous gain, for losing a last baby tooth means a visit from Queen Toothiana.

Toothiana, who can transform herself into mini selves, has also been bestowed with the power of flight, and children all over the land eagerly await her arrival when they've lost a tooth. For baby teeth contain memories, and Toothiana collects them, leaving a surprise—a coin, or a small gem—under the child's pillow in exchange. While Katherine is interested in the surprise, what she really wants to know is her earliest memories. Maybe then she will learn something about her parents, at last. But Toothiana also lost her parents when she was young, in a way most distressing, and how that happened will affect all of the Guardians' futures.

In Which We See the Extremely Secret Process by Which a Tooth Is Gathered

FOR CENTURY UPON CENTURY Queen Toothiana flew majestically on her nightly rounds with her half dozen mini-selves. At the bedside of every child who had left a tooth under his pillow, one of her selves quietly collected the tooth and made a silent wish. The children each were different, but the wish was the same: that the child would grow up to be kind and happy. In the many villages and cities and jungles of Asia, the children knew to place their lost teeth under their pillows. Then a tiny treasure would be left in place of the tooth. And the tooth would be stored in the palace of the flying elephant of Punjam Hy Loo until it was needed again.

Once, Toothiana had loved to spend time at each child's bedside—straightening a blanket that had been kicked off or whispering messages of hope into sleeping ears. She had loved to peek from the windows as the children woke in the morning; their joyful cries when they reached under their pillows and found their gifts—this was *her* treasure.

But she wanted to help all the children in the world, however there simply wasn't enough of her to go around. Since she'd learned long ago that jewels of any kind were likely to bring the wrong kind of interest from adults, she had begun to use coins or other smaller treasures in exchange for teeth. But, oh, the coins! Children loved to receive them; however, as more countries were formed, more currencies were invented, and each child required the coin from his or her realm. It became a complicated business. Even with six of her, there was barely time to outrun the coming dawn.

Yet despite Queen Toothiana's hurried pace, there was something about her presence that calmed every child she visited. And while on any given night she might encounter a bad dream or two, the terrible time of the Nightmare Man seemed to be over. The children in her lands, like children everywhere, called him the Boogeyman, and she'd seen no sign of him for months.

While Queen Toothiana knew less about the Guardians than they knew about her, she'd observed that glimmering boy made of light who had been involved in battling the Boogeyman. She'd seen how brave he'd been saving the girl who wrote stories and drew pictures. She felt a special fondness for the two of them. In a strange way their devotion to each other reminded her of her parents' devotion, and so she was looking very much forward to the last stop of the evening.

For the very first time, she'd received a call to the highest peak in the Himalayas—to the Lunar Lamadary. There, she knew she would find out more about this valiant girl who rode on a giant goose.

Meanwhile, Nightlight waited for Queen Toothiana on the top of the Lamadary's tower with as much patience as he could muster. He remembered the first time he had seen the bird woman: He'd been playing moonbeam tag when she'd flickered by so quickly that he mistook her for an enormous hummingbird. And from time to time they glimpsed each other. She'd never spoken to him, but she always nodded whenever their flying paths briefly crossed. But Nightlight, with his keen intuition, sensed that she distrusted most people and didn't want the other Guardians to know about her, so he had kept his knowledge of her to himself. Besides, there was something about her that made him feel sort of shy.

But Katherine asked for his help. So he kept his eyes trained on the night sky, peering among the bright stars for the first sign of this Toothiana.

Soon, Nightlight spied a glow. It was a shimmer— flickering sparks of iridescent blues and greens. As it came closer, Nightlight made out a feathered head, bright green eyes, and a happy smile. He tried to hide, but Toothiana and her mini-selves saw him before he could leap into the shadows.

Toothiana knew immediately that he was up to

something. Through the centuries, too many children had plotted and planned to wake at the moment she arrived for her to be caught unawares now. She shook her head sternly and held a finger to her lips, warning him not to interfere.

Nightlight wavered. His deepest loyalty rested with Katherine, and yet he found himself acutely aware that he needed to trust this winged being. At least for the moment. With the slightest of nods, he let her know that he would do as she asked. But he followed her closely as she and her selves shot through the window and down to Katherine's bed.

Three of the mini-selves, no bigger than sparrows, each carried a gold coin. They flew silently to Katherine's pillow, then tucked in their wings and crawled gently and silently under it. Another landed by Katherine's ear and plucked at a tiny silver instrument

while she sang a soft, lulling song. Nightlight was fascinated. *They sing to make her sleep more soundly*, he realized.

Another mini-self stood guard by the pillow while the last one winged about the room and seemed to be keeping watch as Toothiana, an expectant smile upon her face, waited for the tooth to be smuggled from under the pillow.

The pillow puckered here and rumpled there, then, at last, the three small fairies emerged, Katherine's tooth in hand. Toothiana picked it up tenderly. With her other hand, she brought out a beautiful, carved, ruby box from a pouch she wore around her neck, and held it tightly.

She closed her eyes as if in deep thought. A glow began to emanate from both Katherine's tooth and the box. The queen's magical power seemed to be working.

Nightlight had seen all he needed. As willful as the flying woman seemed, he would do as Katherine asked. He readied himself to swoop in to take the tooth, but a quiet, mournful sigh from Toothiana made him pause, puzzled. A sadness came over her lovely face, and then her mini-selves sighed as well, as though they shared her every feelings. She could see all of Katherine's memories.

Toothiana murmured, "Poor child. You're like me—you've lost your mother and father. But . . . you didn't even have a chance to know or remember them." She bowed her head ever so slightly and looked down at Katherine, who slept on.

"I must give you the memory you long for," she whispered. Nightlight leaned forward anxiously as Toothiana lowered the hand that held the tooth to Katherine's forehead.

Nightlight knew he needn't steal the tooth now. Katherine would have the memory. He was glad. He felt a peculiar bond with this bird royal and didn't want to anger her.

But suddenly, a sound most angry stopped Toothiana from granting Katherine her wish.

Monkey See, Monkey Don't

Monkeys, dozens of them, sprang through the windows of Katherine's room and swarmed the chamber. They were huge, hulking, and armed with daggers, spears, and crude weapons.

What is this dark business? Toothiana wondered in shock as a handful of the malicious creatures, screeching loudly, leaped upon her with a swiftness that was unnatural. She crammed the ruby box back into its pouch, then turned, batting her wings at the fiends as she tried to escape their grip, then drew her swords and slashed away. But the monkeys were too quick.

Katherine startled awake and instinctively grabbed for the dagger on her night table as six or eight of her attackers grasped her arms and legs. A monkey with a grotesquely humanlike face pressed his hand against her mouth so that she could not cry out. Nightlight was there in a flash, batting the animals away with his staff, but for each monkey he hit, seven would take its place. The room was overrun with chattering, maniacal monster monkeys.

Queen Toothiana knew she had to protect the girl. As Katherine struggled to free herself, Toothiana lunged for the monkeys. In the tangle of tails and clawing hands, Katherine's tooth was knocked to the floor. Both Toothiana and Katherine cried out at the same time.

Katherine was determined not to lose that tooth. She elbowed one monkey after another, reaching,

reaching, reaching for the tooth. Each time her fingers nearly gripped it, it was kicked away. Katherine darted along the floor on her hands and knees, her eyes never leaving the tooth. Finally, it was within her grasp. One great last stretch, then—got it!

Only then, when her precious tooth was safely tucked in her palm, did Katherine think to scream, to call out for help. She didn't get a chance. Once again a hand covered her mouth. Then another had her leg; another, her arm.

Katherine strained against her captors, trying to squirm away as Toothiana and Nightlight struck at monkey after monkey. The tiny versions of Toothiana dove and charged relentlessly at the primates' eyes. They were making headway when a second wave of monkeys attacked. There were just too many.

The largest monkey, the one who seemed the

leader, snatched the pouch from around Toothiana's neck, raised it over his head, and hurled it to one of his minions, who promptly leaped out the window with the prize, followed by a dark mass of his scuffling cohorts.

Toothiana struggled to follow them, sweeping her wings at the monkeys in her way, but then she stopped short. The monkey who had taken her precious box—she recognized him! *That vile creature . . . That monkey was the one who . . .* Toothiana's rage took hold, and in one swift move, she had him in her grip.

The room became a cyclone of monkeys; they stampeded around the walls and began to bound out the windows in waves. They seemed to be running right across the night sky, as if it had become solid under their feet. And then in a flash of darkness, the monkeys vanished.

All except one.

Toothiana pressed her sword against her old enemy's throat, breathing hard.

The door flew open. North burst into the room, with Ombric, Bunnymund, Yaloo and his Yeti lieutenants, and even a few sleepy-eyed Lamas right behind him.

"Villains, explain yourselves!" North demanded, his cutlass ready.

Toothiana didn't respond. Nor did she remove her blade from the monkey's neck.

North took a step closer, and Toothiana cocked her head, birdlike, from right to left. As North took another step, her feathers flared up, as if to warn him not to come closer. One of her wings hung limp.

The captive monkey, frantic-eyed, whimpered something that sounded vaguely like "Help!"

Everyone froze, wonderstruck at the sight of the flying woman they had heard so much about. They had expected a serene being, but here she was in fighting stance and with a death grip on a decidedly evil-looking ape. Ombric was madly sorting through the various dialects of primate languages to best question the captive monkey. *Odd how humanlike it looks*, he thought. *Very odd indeed.*

In all the confusion, it was Nightlight who was the first to notice that Katherine was not in her bed.

Before he could alert the others, they all felt the surge of his frantic worry.

North whipped his head back and forth, surveying the room. "Katherine?" he called. Then "KATHERINE!" Dread crept through the Guardians when there came no reply.

Ombric and Bunnymund reached out to her with

their minds, but they got only a confusing darkness in response.

North turned his attention back to Toothiana and the strange creatures she held prisoner. He glared menacingly at them, raising his sword.

"Tell me what you've done with Katherine," he demanded, "or you will never take another breath."

A Journey Most Confounding, with Flying Monkeys Who Smell Very Badly Indeed

KATHERINE CLUTCHED HER TOOTH as she tried to push away the putrid cloak that one of the monkeys had thrown over her head. The last thing she had seen had been the monkey with the humanlike face take Toothiana's pouch. Then it dawned on her. *That must be the Monkey King from Toothiana's story!*

The air felt colder, so Katherine knew she had been dragged outside. Her mind raced with so many questions, she hardly had time to be scared. *The Monkey King has come for revenge, but why take me?* she wondered. She felt herself being prodded and shoved and sometimes even thrown from one tight grip to another, speeding along at an impossibly fast pace. The monkeys seemed to be running on solid ground, but sometimes it felt like they were—what? Flying? She pulled at the cloak till she made a small hole. Clouds. Stars. Sky. They *were* flying! And were extremely high.

At that moment the cloak slipped to one side, and Katherine caught a glimpse of solid surface below—a road made of shadows. She gasped. It was like Nightlight's roads of light, but inky and frightening. *There's only one being who could make a sky road of shadows*, she realized with dread.

And then she remembered her dream, her awful dream.

Screeching incessantly, the monkeys sped on. Katherine tried to reach out to her friends with her mind, but something about this dark highway was blocking her thoughts.

Her breath formed tiny icicles around her face and nose as freezing air rushed past. She ripped the hole bigger and was finally able to take a deep, unfettered breath, but it was too cold, and she pulled the cloak shut, now feeling smothered again.

The monkeys had a stink to them that she hadn't expected; they'd looked much sweeter in the pictures from Ombric's ancient book. A fleeting wish that she had taken the time to learn the language of monkeys flashed through her mind. Ombric could speak it, no doubt, but as there were no monkeys in Santoff Claussen, it had seemed much more important to learn languages she could actually use—like squirrel and Lunar Moth. She could likely learn it easily enough. She'd learned Great Snow Goose, hadn't she?

Oh, Kailash! Katherine thought with a groan. *She will be so worried. Nightlight, too.* Then it struck her: What if he were wounded? A wave of fear for her friends swept over her, forcing her attention back to the dilemma at hand. She kicked and pushed against the cloak, but it was futile. The monkeys simply held it tighter around her, until she could barely move her arms.

The temperature was changing again, slowly at first and then more quickly. The icy air warmed. The cloak felt suffocating. Katherine's stomach lurched as the monkeys took a giant leap and then bounced up and down on what felt like a tree branch.

The cloak slipped from her head. This time the monkeys made no effort to cover her face as they swung from tree to tree, dragging Katherine along with them. Sometimes it seemed the branches could never hold them, and then they'd plummet down, down, down, in rapid falls, leaves slapping at Katherine's face and neck. She found herself being thrown from one paw to the next until one of the monkeys would grab a solid branch and begin the ascent again.

Besides the screeching monkeys—were they *ever* quiet?—Katherine saw no other jungle creatures at all, not even birds. It was as if the monkeys were the only animals in this land. *Where are the other animals?* she wondered. *Where are the elephants and the tigers? The snakes and the lizards?*

And then, without warning, the monkeys let go of their grasp and dropped Katherine. She didn't fall far. Just a few feet. When she realized she was unhurt, she began to cautiously look around. She could not see much beneath the jungle canopy, but she was able to pick out what seemed to be the ruins of what once must have been a magnificent city. The jungle had done its best to take it over, but Katherine could see evidence of the city's former glory in the tarnished gold and silver fixtures on the crumbling walls.

Where in the world am I? She looked in every direction and didn't see a soul, just the army of monkeys. But now they kept their distance. It had become eerily quiet. So Katherine decided there was nothing to do but investigate. She headed for the closest buildings, stopping at the first to peer at a dirt-covered mosaic. The design, though half buried under a layer of mud and mold, looked exquisite, so using the side of her fist, she wiped the muck off until she could make out the outline of an elephant—an elephant with wings.

"The flying elephant!" she said with a gasp. *I'm in Punjam Hy Loo!* It seemed almost a dream. Just yesterday Mr. Qwerty had told them all about this city and the Sisters of Flight!

She looked in every direction. *Were the sisters still here somewhere? What has brought this city so low? Were there still elephants guarding the mountain?* She looked for more clues and didn't notice that the shadows around her were growing larger. Blacker. She didn't see that hundreds more monkeys were quietly perching on the derelict walls surrounding her.

It wasn't until an immense shadow loomed directly over her that Katherine looked up and gulped. It was as she feared.

"Pitch," she said, trying to sound calm.

The Nightmare King greeted her with a ghoulish smile. "Greetings, my Darkling Daughter," he whispered in a voice that was anything but welcoming.

Panic in the Himalayas

WHERE IS KATHERINE?" NORTH roared again at the winged woman in front of him. He was sure she had some hand in Katherine's disappearance, but his sword was pulling away from this strange being—he'd almost forgotten how the sword, the first relic from the Man in the Moon, could tell friend from foe. The sword knew Toothiana meant no harm to any Guardian. But North resisted it. The woman knew something, and she must tell them.

Nightlight sat on Katherine's bed. Her pillow had been tossed to the floor, but the three coins that had been left for her were still in place.

Toothiana's eyes darted from North to the others, one hand still tight around the struggling monkey's neck, the other still clasping her sword, poised and ready to end this creature's life. With a quick glance, she told her mini-selves to stay back. Her feathers fluffed and quivered. *With rage?* North wondered. *Or panic?*

He had seen that look before. As a boy in the wild, he had known it well. It was the look of a trapped animal, one that had nothing to lose, so would go down fighting. North had learned how to approach them—calmly and carefully.

Then it dawned on North how he and the others must appear to her—this queen who had every reason to mistrust adults. She was facing a sword-wielding warrior, a seven-foot-tall bunny, an ancient wizard, and Abominable Snowmen bearing all manner of weapons. The set of Toothiana's jaw was fierce, but her eyes, almond-shaped and green, betrayed her. *Why, she must feel just like a sparrow caught in a cage,* he thought.

So North held up one hand and sheathed his sword. He approached the queen slowly. Even the monkey stopped his squirming as North took one careful step after another, never blinking, never taking his eyes off her.

"We mean you no harm," North said in his most soothing voice. "But we are most anxious to find our friend—the girl you were here to see tonight. Do you know what happened to her?"

Toothiana cocked her head, held North's gaze in her own for the longest time, then seemed to make a decision: She would trust this hulking man.

"Gone. Taken," she said.

"Taken where? By whom?" North encouraged, forcing his voice to stay steady.

"*This* creature knows," she said, gesturing toward the monkey.

Ombric made one cautious step forward. "Is that creature the Monkey King?" he asked, recalling Toothiana's story.

She nodded, then gave the creature a hard shake. "Tell what you know!"

The monkey spat at her. "Never!" he screeched.

North could scarcely contain himself. "Tell us!" he roared. "Or die!"

The monkey merely sucked on his teeth and smirked.

Toothiana grabbed the simian by his feet and swung him upside down, giving him a good shake with each word. "Where. Is. The. Girl? Where. Is. My. Box?"

"Gone. Taken," the Monkey King mimicked.

North unsheathed his sword and brought its tip to the monkey's chin.

The Monkey King simply continued to suck on his teeth, as if being held upside down with a sword pressed to his chin was a perfectly normal course of events.

Bunnymund's whiskers bristled. He, too, knew the ways of animals, even better than North did. And North—like all poor humans—was beginning to let his emotions get the best of him. It was time for cooler heads. It was time for the Pooka to take charge.

He pressed a paw on North's arm until North lowered his sword. Then he eyed the monkey appraisingly. "You're very clever," the Pooka told him. "Clever enough to fool all of us. To break into the Lamadary. To lead your troops to capture our friend. And steal this lady's precious treasure."

While he was talking, he was pulling a chocolate egg out of his pocket and carefully peeling it, as one would a piece of fruit. The aroma of a perfectly ripe banana, tinged with the scent of milky chocolate, filled the room.

Bunnymund motioned to Toothiana to turn the monkey right side up again. As she did, the monkey's eyes began to gleam. He reached for the chocolate, which Bunnymund dropped into his hand. Popping the confection into his mouth, the Monkey King closed his eyes. "Yum-yum," he said blissfully.

Nightlight watched closely. He had never before wanted to harm a creature of flesh and blood. Pitch was darkness, a phantom, but the monkey man was *alive*—a living being. Nightlight saw the hate in Toothiana's eyes for this creature. And in North's. Even Ombric's. And now he felt it too. And he did not like it.

The Monkey King motioned for another chocolate as Nightlight fought the urge to spear him through with his staff.

"What a wise monkey king. You want more. And more you'll have," Bunnymund said, patting his pockets and backing away. "But first you must answer our questions."

The Monkey King bobbed his head up and down

and answered in the language of monkeys.

Ombric translated. "The King of the Monkeys claims he is much too clever to fall for our tricks."

The monkey's eyes widened. He had never before met a human who could speak monkey.

"You are indeed clever, Maharaja," Ombric said, "but perhaps not as clever as you think you are. Who sent you to kidnap our friend?"

"No one sent me," the monkey said, speaking in the language of men. He raised his head haughtily. "I am a king. I lead my army where I choose. I am not 'sent.' And now I demand to be fed."

"Some army," North scoffed. "They've left you behind."

"They have not!" he howled.

"Then where oh where have they gone?" asked Bunnymund.

No longer a maharajah,
the Monkey King is maha-rose.

The Monkey King stiffened. "They'll be back."

Bunnymund took out another chocolate with a flourish and held it close to the Monkey King's nose.

"You'll get no more answers from me, *Rabbit Man*," the Monkey King spat.

"Then no more yummies for you," said Bunnymund. He handed the chocolate to Ombric, who peeled tantalizingly, then bit it in half. The banana-laced fragrance filled the room.

The monkey eyed the other half of the chocolate and whimpered, "More yum-yum." Bunnymund shook his head.

"I *can't* tell you," the Monkey King whimpered. "I will be killed until dead."

"Who would dare do such a thing to such a clever Monkey King?" Ombric asked, searching for an even tone, though alarm bells were exploding in his head.

The Monkey King saw a chance to bargain. He drew himself up again. "One who can make me human again—make me much, much maharaja. Can *you* do that?"

North was growing tired of this back-and-forth. The longer this went on, the farther away Katherine could be taken. He leaped forward and smashed the monkey onto the floor. "Tell us what we ask!" he demanded.

The monkey giggled and pointed at Toothiana. "In *her* home. They wait at Punjam Hy Loo."

Toothiana trembled with rage. "You lie!"

"No, no, no," cackled the monkey. " 'Tis all part of the plan!"

"Coward!" North spat out, pacing in front of him. "You're a pathetic excuse for a king."

"And always have been," Toothiana added.

The Monkey King scowled darkly, his anger building. "Wait until the King of Nightmares makes me the King of Mans again. I will kill you deader than your father!"

Toothiana pulled her sword to his head. How dare he boast of such things in her presence!

But North and the other Guardians barely noticed. The words "King of Nightmares" had stilled them. North ceased pacing; Nightlight glowed brightly. Bunnymund's whiskers twitched, and Ombric's beard began to curl with worry. They all had only one thought.

Pitch was back!

"What does the Nightmare King want with my ruby box?" Toothiana asked now.

"And why take Katherine and leave the rest of us?" North demanded.

The Monkey King's eyes gleamed with triumph. "He seeks to build an army. And turn the girl into his Darkling Princess."

In Which Toothiana Makes a Startling Discovery

INSTANTLY THE GUARDIANS BEGAN to talk in low, tense voices. Queen Toothiana, however, kept her eyes trained on the Monkey King.

The Monkey King looked back at her with a gloat of self-importance.

Toothiana's eyes narrowed; her anger felt venomous. She thought about all of her years on the run. About her parents' deaths. Every sorrow of her life had been caused by this pathetic monkey.

He tried to avert her gaze, but Toothiana grabbed him by the neck again and forced him to look at her.

"How?" she demanded. "How did the jungle law spare you?"

The Monkey King glared at her, his eyes matching her own in the fury they contained. "The tigers tore at me. The serpents bit me. Every creature gave me wounds, but I would not die, for I had to destroy . . . YOU!"

"My father *saved* you," said Toothiana.

The Monkey King glanced away, drawing in a shaky breath.

Toothiana wondered if there was anything about this monkey worth sparing. Her father had saved him once, and he had been repaid with angry mobs and an early death. Did this monkey maharaja have even a shred of his childlike goodness left? There was only one way to know for sure. With an angry cry, Toothiana pried open the Monkey King's mouth.

"No baby teeth!" she shouted. "You die."

The monkey yowled, wrenching his jaw from her hands.

Toothiana swung her sword to strike a deadly blow when North bounded across the room and grabbed her wrist.

"No!" he yelled. "We need the creature. He can help us rescue our friend."

She scoffed at him. This monkey would never help anyone but himself. She lowered her sword.

"I'll leave," she said. "For Punjam Hy Loo. I'll get the ruby box *and* your girl."

"Pitch—he's crueler and more devious than you'd ever imagine," North warned. "You can't go alone."

"We'll come with you," Ombric implored. "Together our power is mighty."

Toothiana scoffed again. "This Pitch scares me not

at all." With that, she leaped onto the windowsill and prepared to spring into the air. But as she spread her wings, she listed to the left. Her right wing, her beautiful, iridescent right wing, hung limp.

Nightlight Sees a Woman of Mystery

KATHERINE TRAPPED AND ALONE with the Nightmare King was the worst thing Nightlight could possibly imagine.

For a new fear gripped him, one that he could not describe even to himself, for it was a feeling beyond his own understanding. But he knew that Katherine longed for a father's love and that Pitch had lost a daughter. Could this be a dangerous thing for his friend? He thought of what he'd seen in the Dream Tear and shook his head.

As he sat at the tower top, he looked up to the

Moon for reassurance, but it was blocked by dense, fast-moving clouds. There was a strange wind blowing, and Nightlight couldn't shake the feeling that he was being watched; even that his thoughts were somehow overheard. He'd had this feeling before. It was only when he was alone, and it did not seem threatening—but it was strange. He sometimes thought he saw a face—a woman's face, for just an instant—in the shapes of the clouds or in a swirl of leaves that blew past him or even in a mist of falling snowflakes. He never saw it clearly, and he wondered if it was just his daydreaming ways that made him think he even glimpsed this woman, but this time he looked about, trying to see if she was really there. He knew he felt something. He knew it felt tied somehow to Katherine and Pitch. He let his thoughts reach out, as they could with Katherine, but there was no response.

Just a vague feeling that someone, not unfriendly, was watching and waiting.

Nightlight paced about nervously. He needed to calm down, he needed a moment of peace, for his mind was not ready for all these strange feelings and grown-up thoughts. He didn't know what to do. How could he help Katherine? Should he fly pell-mell into the unknown and try to save her on his own? He was brave and clever enough—but this time he felt that it would take more than he could manage. He thought of the Bird Lady, Toothiana, this queen with a mother's heart and a warrior's ways—maybe she would know the trick of saving Katherine. But her wing was hurting and she could not fly.

Then he thought of Kailash. The Snow Goose rarely slept without Katherine by her side, but on this night she had stayed in her old nest, among the Snow Geese she hadn't seen in so very long. Kailash loved Katherine as much as he did. Kailash! Suddenly Nightlight had an idea that was both childish and knowing.

The children of Santoff Claussen huddled with Kailash in the nesting cave. The terrible news of Katherine's abduction had reached every corner of the Lamadary.

When Nightlight arrived at the cave, he found Tall William doing his best to appear brave and strong while Sascha and Petter readied a saddle. The children had decided to try and save Katherine themselves while riding Kailash. Nightlight knew better than to laugh or scold them for attempting this impossible mission.

He reached over to Kailash and gently stroked

her feathers. She gave a low, woeful honk, then rested her head on Nightlight's slender shoulder.

He knew his idea would work. He gathered the geese and the children together.

And so began a strange parade—Nightlight, followed by a dozen or so children and a flock of Giant Snow Geese, made their way through the Lamadary, past Yetis who were sharpening weapons in preparation for a great battle, past Lunar Lamas who were thumbing through their ancient books looking for clues that might help Katherine, and past the villagers from Santoff Claussen, who were standing about in worried clumps, sharing ideas and comforts. They didn't stop, not even to answer Old William's question about where they were going, until they reached Katherine's room.

They found Queen Toothiana there. Her back

was toward them—one of her iridescent wings dangled limply.

North was asking her in a gentle yet urgent voice, "And why in the world would Pitch come after you?"

Toothiana answered; her voice had a low cooing quality. "When I'd left the Monkey King, I flew up to Punjam Hy Loo. I found my mother's sisters, the Sisters of Flight. They had been waiting for me! But as they greeted me, they seemed so very sad. They asked of my mother. When I told them of her death, their leader sighed. 'We felt it, we thought it, now we know it to be true,' she told me." Toothiana's own eyes filled with tears, but she continued.

"The sisters formed a circle around the flying elephant, and one by one—right in front of me!—they turned into wood, like carved statues. Branches began to grow from them, branches that weaved themselves together like a giant basket. And as the last sister began to stiffen and change, she said to me, 'If one of us dies, we all die; you are queen here now. You must tend the elephant. He will protect all the memories of us, the memories of everything.'" Toothiana's one strong wing flapped ever more quickly.

"The elephant never forgets," Toothiana told them again. "It is he who touched the fabled Magic Tooth my parents bequeathed me. It is he who saw the memories that dwelled inside."

"But whose tooth is it?" asked Ombric in a hushed tone.

"The one who lives in the Moon," she answered.

The Lunar Lamas all murmured at once with excitement. "The tooth of the Man in the Moon!"

"Astounding!" said Ombric. "Toothiana has one of the five relics."

North needed to know more. "But what power does it bestow, Your Highness?"

"With it I can see the memories within the teeth. And once, when I was caged by this royal primate," she said, pointing her sword at the Monkey King, who was now bound by heavy shackles and chains, "I asked it to help me. It was then that I became more than I am. That is when there was more of me."

As if to explain better, the six mini-versions of Toothiana fluttered down from their perches in the candelabra that hung from the ceiling. They landed on Toothiana's shoulders, three on each side, and bowed.

Ombric pulled at his beard, thinking. This he had *never* seen. "Pitch could make much mischief if he were able to use that relic—maybe even harness the power of the flying elephant," he told them uneasily.

Nightlight felt a cold chill. Sascha, standing in the doorway beside him, couldn't help herself. She gasped, and Toothiana and the others spun around. The queen was even grander than the children had imagined. Her wings—they were magnificent—the most beautiful shades of blues and greens. Her eyes were as bright as a bird's, and her headdress was as glorious as any peacock's. And she was covered in a layer of tiny green and blue feathers that caught the light like prisms and filled the room with tiny reflected rainbows.

As the children stood, staring in awe, Kailash and one of the other Snow Geese stepped forward, honking. Kailash went on for quite some time. Toothiana's expression lit up when she learned that they could fix her wing, for she was, of course, fluent in all the bird languages, Snow Goose being a particular favorite.

Ombric placed a hand on North's arm. "Come, it's time to leave the queen to her helpers," he told him. "She's suffered a terrible injury and needs time to recover."

"We must rescue Katherine now!" said North. "Every second counts."

Bunnymund shook his head. He, too, was nearly desperate with worry about Katherine, but he would never let his emotions take over. Why, that would make him practically *human*. "I'll dig a tunnel to wherever we need to go, but first it would be most advantageous to know what to expect when we get there, and whether or not chocolate eggs will be required."

North had been in too many battles in his young life to ignore the sense in Bunnymund's words. He reluctantly agreed, but that didn't mean he was finished questioning the monkey. He grabbed him by the arm and dragged him toward the door, followed by Ombric and Bunnymund. "We'll be back," he called to Toothiana.

The Snow Geese, now cooing, began repairing the queen's damaged wing. Nightlight and the children stayed out of the way, watching the miraculous work of the geese. With unimaginable delicacy, they twined and smoothed each strand of Toothiana's crumpled feathers, layer after layer after layer. And slowly, the wing began to look as good as new.

The queen gave the injured wing a slight flutter. "Still hurts," she said, "but it is much better." Then she cocked her head from side to side, eyeing the children. "You should be asleep."

William the Absolute Youngest shook his head. "We're worried about our friend," he said.

Toothiana nodded, giving her repaired wing another careful flutter. She perched on the edge of Katherine's bed, turning her full attention to the children. Her very presence soothed them, just as it did the sleeping children she visited every night.

The youngest William now ventured a small smile. "We live in Santoff Claussen," he told her.

"It's the best village in the whole world," Sascha added. Then she gave a shiver. "Except for when the Nightmare King comes to visit."

The children began to tell Toothiana all about

their magical village and about the first time that Pitch's Fearlings had attacked them in the forest. "It was Katherine— She was the bravest, and she saved us," Tall William said.

"And that's when we first saw Nightlight!" his youngest brother added.

Petter, Fog, and the others acted out the various battles they'd seen.

Toothiana seemed properly impressed by their derring-do, and so the youngest William ventured to ask for a favor: "Can you—would you—make a wish on my next lost tooth? I don't have any loose ones right now, but you can pull one if you want." He opened his mouth as wide as he could so she could easily choose the best tooth.

"I needn't pull your tooth, but," Toothiana said, trying not to laugh, "name your wish."

"I wish for Katherine to come back to us, safe and sound," said William the Absolute Youngest.

"That's my wish too!" Sascha added.

"And mine," Petter said.

And one by one, the children asked for the same wish: the safe return of Katherine.

Toothiana listened carefully, then told them, "I will try."

Finally, William the Absolute Youngest—who may just have been William the *Wisest*—suggested they recite Ombric's first lesson.

And so, with Toothiana taking Katherine's place in their circle, the children joined hands and recited: "I believe. I believe. I believe."

But Nightlight did not join them. He stood alone. His face was blank and expressionless. Then full of fear.

North burst into the room, pressing through the door just ahead of Ombric and Bunnymund. "The monkey finally talked!" he said.

"We know his plan!" said Ombric.

"To Punjam Hy Loo?" Toothiana asked.

"And right speedily," replied Bunnymund.

Toothiana sprang to her feet, fluttered her wings, and brandished her swords. "Let's fly."

TO BE CONTINUED . . .

To speed the Guardians to Punjam Hy Loo, Queen Toothiana's fallen city, E. Aster Bunnymund eats one of his chocolate eggs in its entirety, which always leads to peculiar reactions. And the result is indeed most astonishing, but even more astonishing is what the Guardians discover when they reach the ruins of the once majestic kingdom—about Pitch, about Katherine, about the Monkey King, and about themselves. For Toothiana and the Guardians want to avenge Katherine and do away with Pitch and the Monkey King once and for all, but at what price?

Find out in the next installment of

TOOTHIANA
A Battle Is Waged